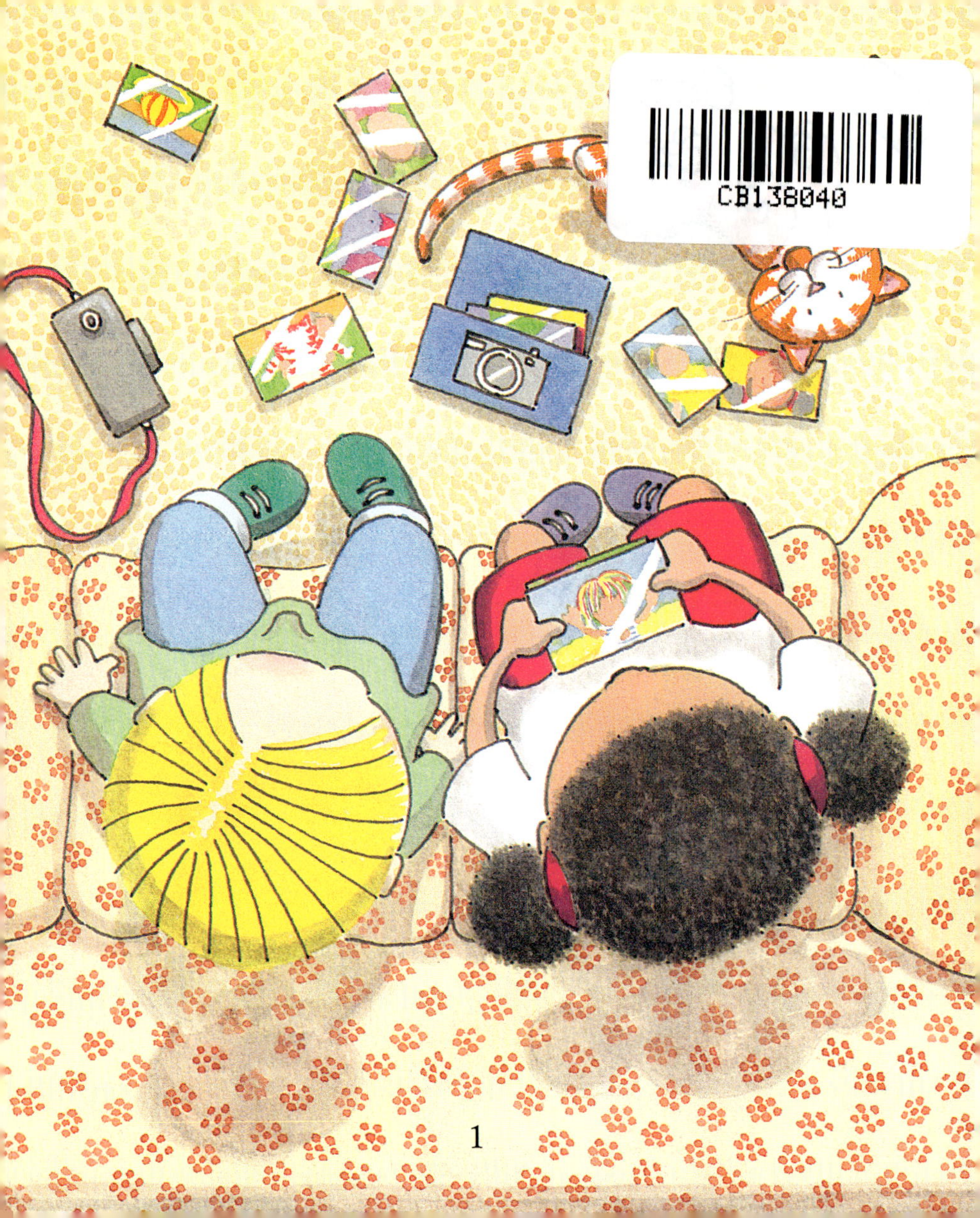

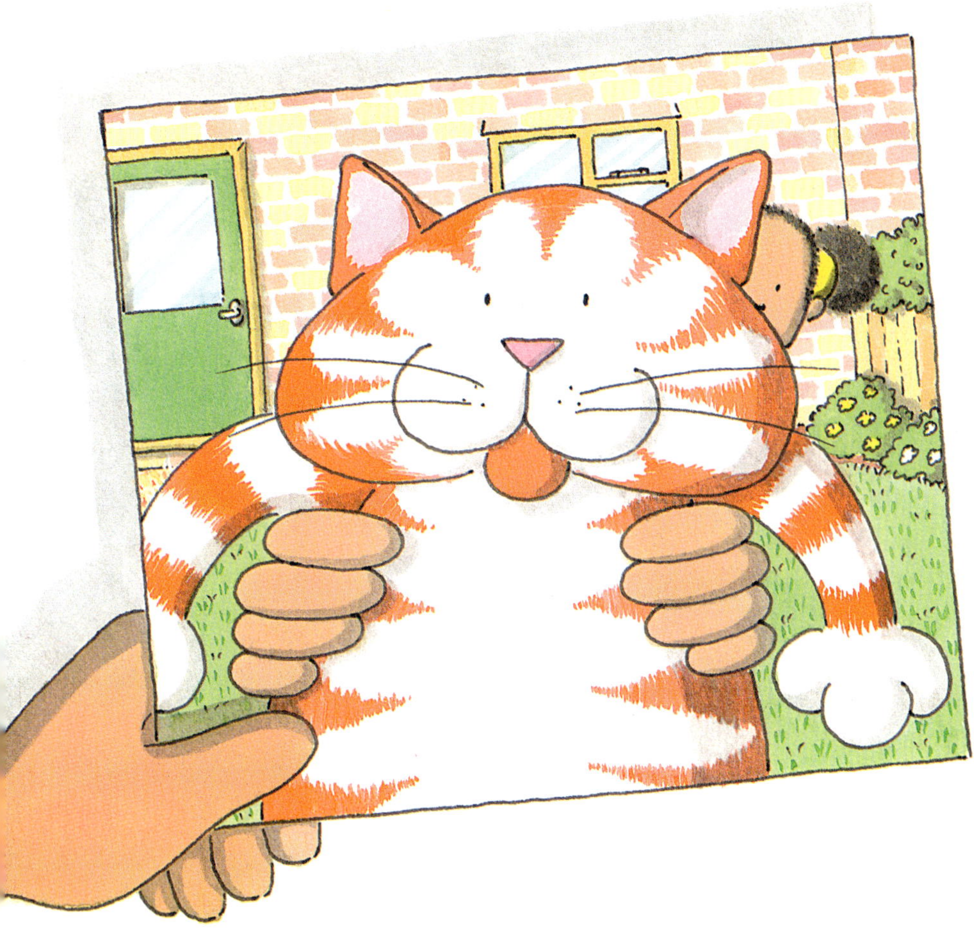

That's me with my cat.

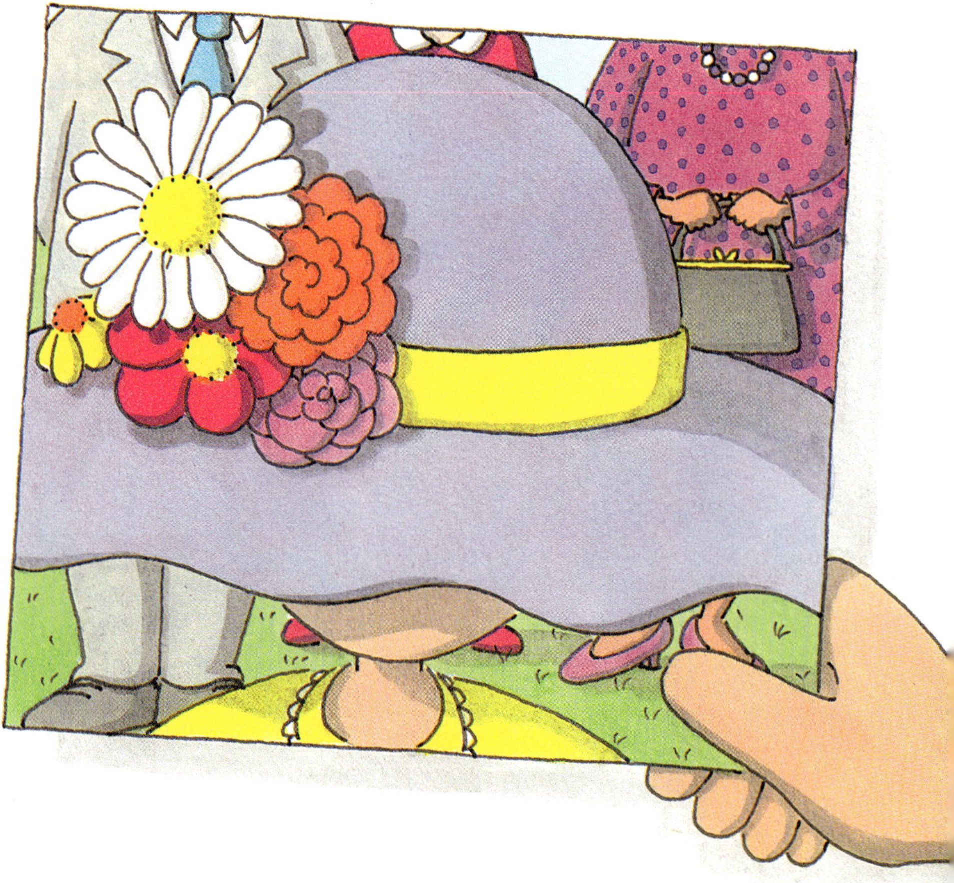

That’s me in Mum’s hat.

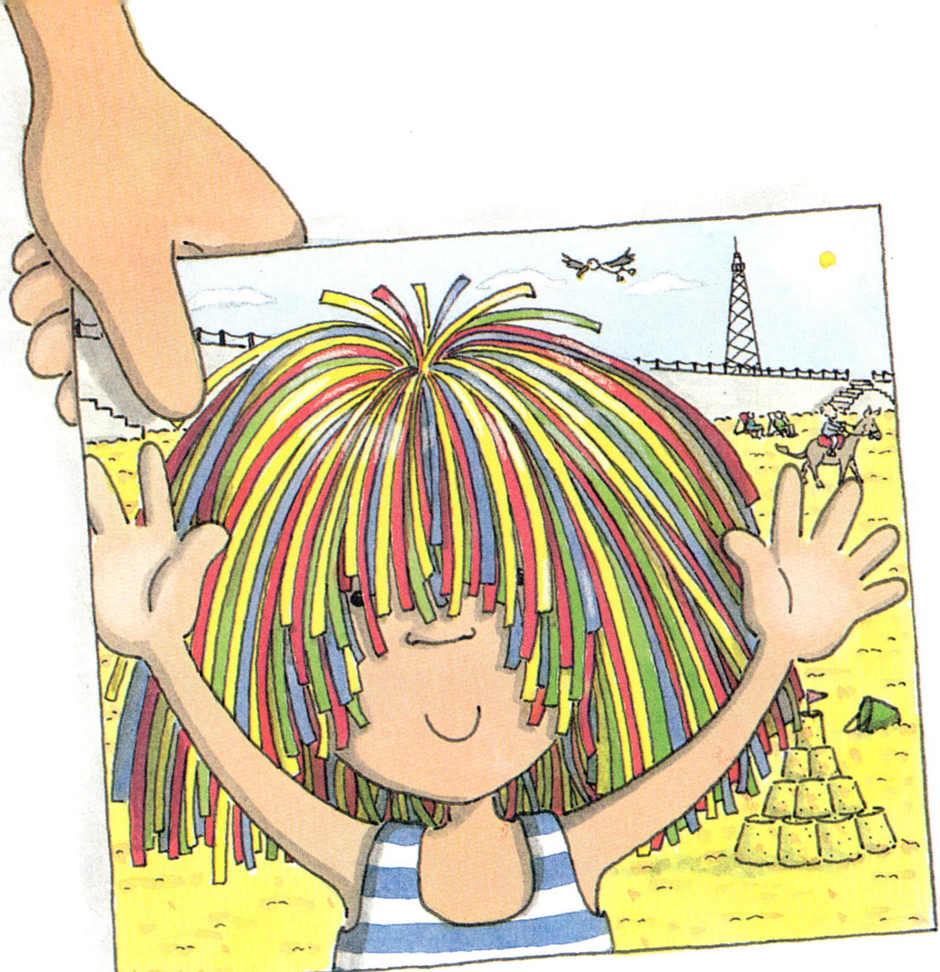

That's me with long hair.

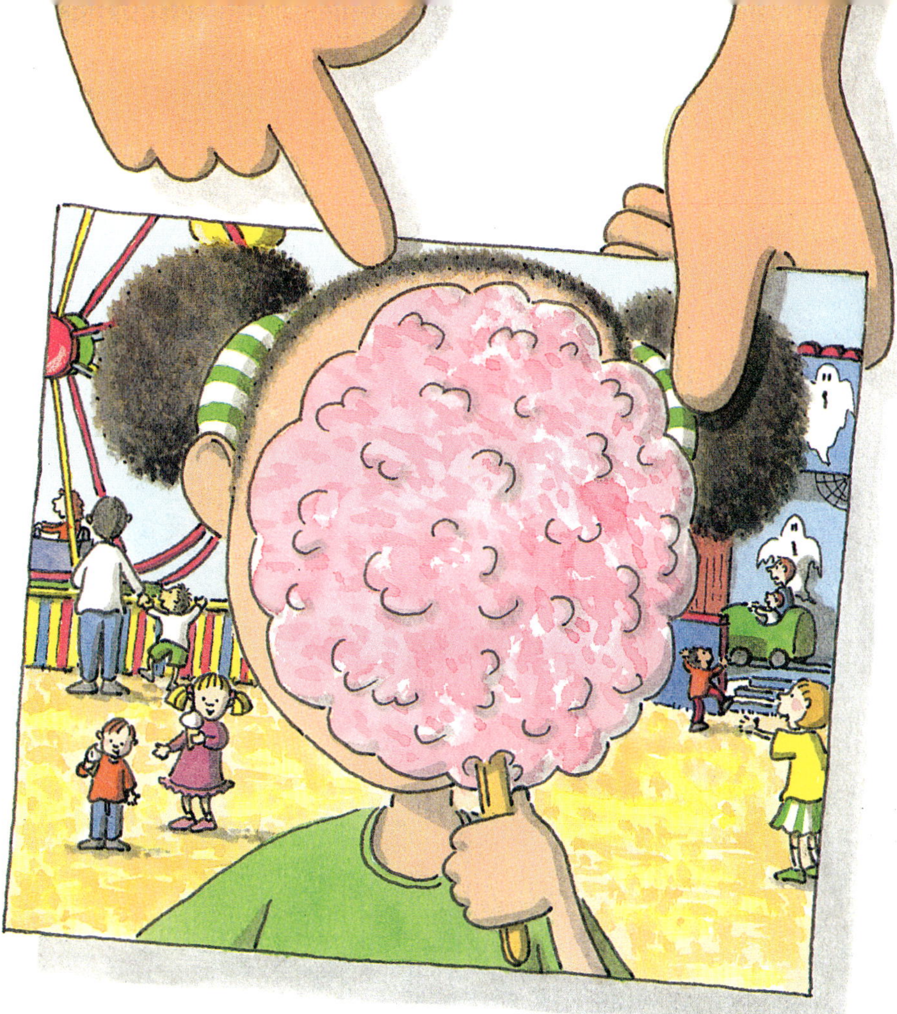

That's me at the fair.

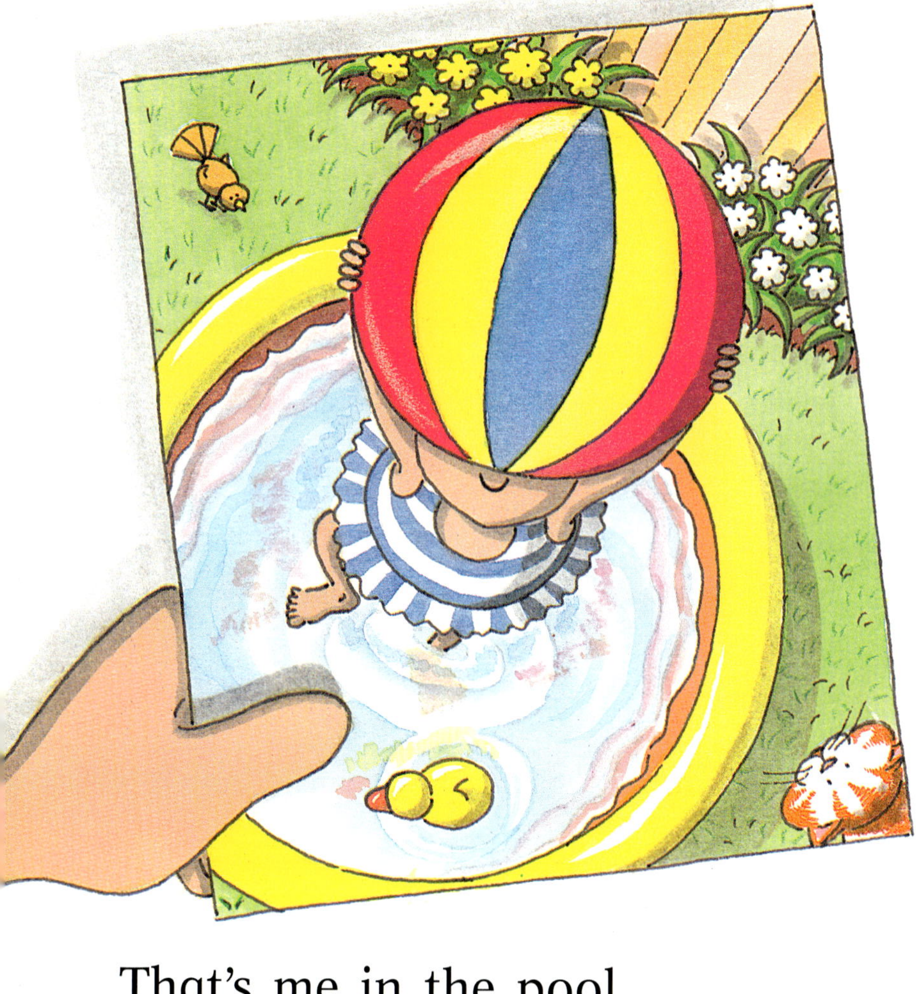

That’s me in the pool.

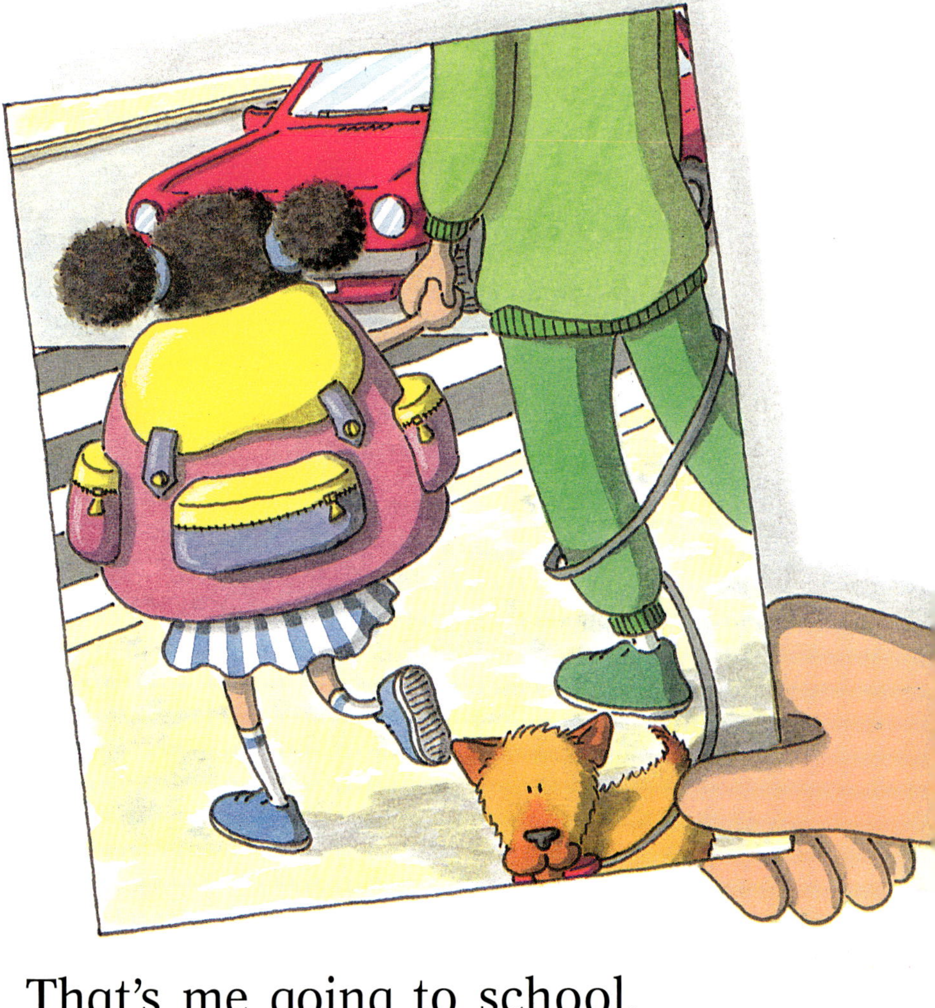

That's me going to school.

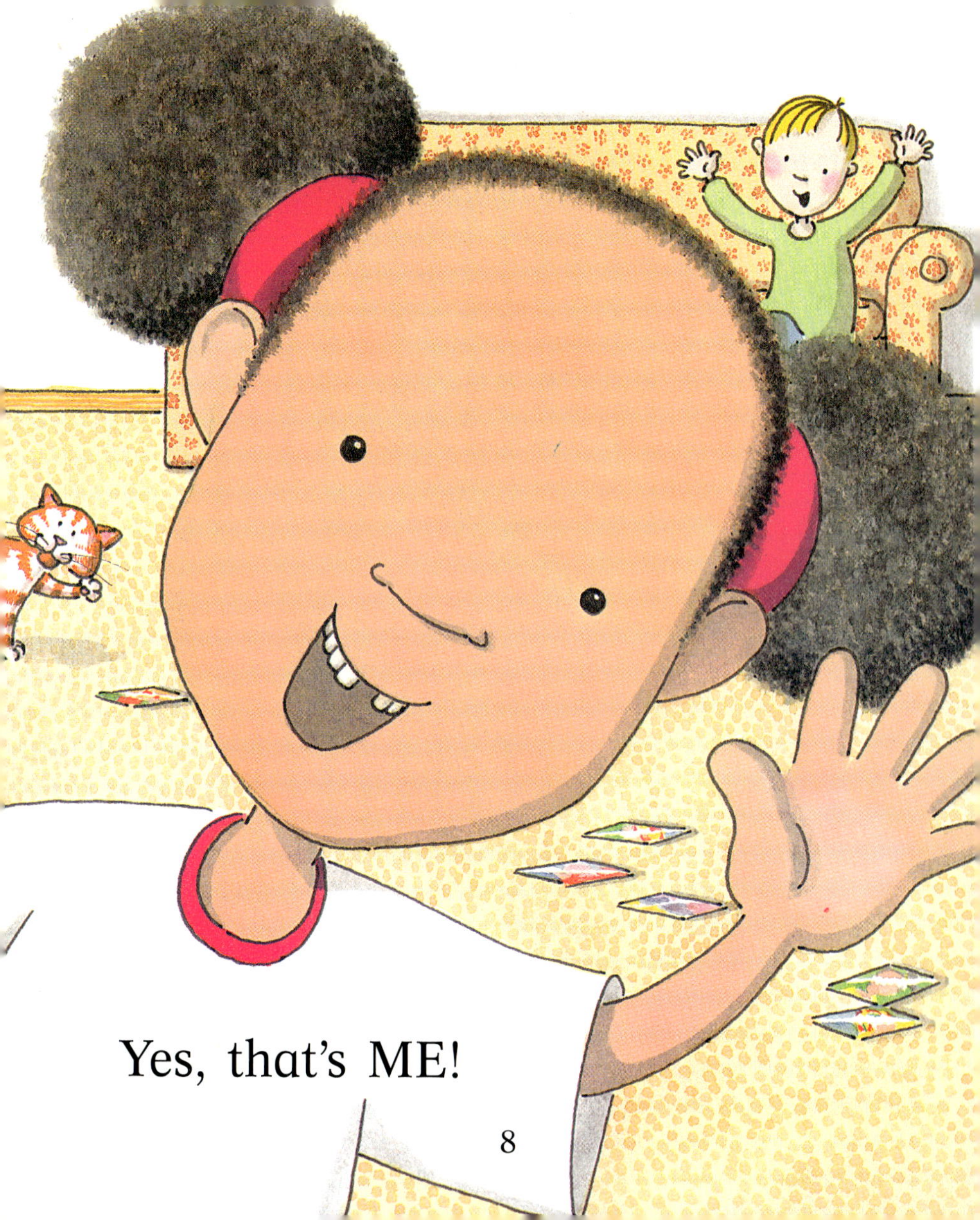

Yes, that's ME!